TIMBERWOLF Tracks

Sigmund Brouwer

illustrated by **Graham Ross**

ORCA BOOK PUBLISHERS

Library and Archives Canada Cataloguing in Publication

Brouwer, Sigmund, 1959-
Timberwolf tracks / written by Sigmund Brouwer.

(Orca echoes)
(Howling Timber Wolves).
ISBN 978-1-55143-734-7

I. Title. II. Series. III. Series: Brouwer, Sigmund, 1959- .
Howling Timber Wolves.
PS8553.R68467T5475 2008 JC813'.54 C2008-903426-0

First published in the United States, 2009
Library of Congress Control Number: 2008930032

Summary: In this sixth book in the Timberwolves series, Johnny Maverick and his friends, Tom and Stu, go on a road trip to the annual fathers-against-sons hockey game.

Orca Book Publishers gratefully acknowledges the support for its publishing programs provided by the following agencies: the Government of Canada through the Canada Book Fund and the Canada Council for the Arts, and the Province of British Columbia through the BC Arts Council and the Book Publishing Tax Credit.

Typesetting by Teresa Bubela
Cover artwork and interior illustrations by Graham Ross
Author photo by Bill Bilsley

ORCA BOOK PUBLISHERS
PO Box 5626, Stn. B
Victoria, BC Canada
V8R 6S4

ORCA BOOK PUBLISHERS
PO Box 468
Custer, WA USA
98240-0468

www.orcabook.com
Printed and bound in Canada.
Printed on 100% PCW recycled paper.

13 12 11 10 • 5 4 3 2

Chapter One
Shoe Check?!

"Shoe check," Johnny Maverick said. He sat at a table in the Billy Goat Café on a Saturday afternoon. It was the only restaurant in the small town of Howling.

"Shoe check?" Tom Morgan echoed. "I've said it before. I'll say it again. This town is a lot different than Toronto."

Johnny and Tom were friends. And teammates. They played hockey for the Howling Timberwolves. Tom used to live in Toronto.

"Sure, Howling is different," Johnny said. "But why do you need to say it again?"

"I've heard of a coat check at a restaurant. But never a shoe check," said Tom.

"Huh?" Johnny said. "In Toronto people put ketchup on coats? That's a mean thing to do. At least you can clean ketchup off shoes without leaving a stain. Who would put ketchup on a coat?"

"Are you nuts?" Tom said. "We don't put ketchup on coats in Toronto."

"But you said coat check." Johnny was frowning at Tom.

"Because you said shoe check," Tom said. "In Toronto you check your coat in at the door. Usually at fancy restaurants. The Billy Goat Café is not fancy. Why would they want you to check your shoes in at the door?"

Johnny thought about what Tom said. Then Johnny smiled.

"You have a lot to learn," Johnny said. "I'm glad Stu and I are able to help you."

Tom frowned. "Where is Stu? I thought he was going to meet us here. He never misses a chance for food."

"Don't worry," Johnny said. "He got here before we did."

Tom looked around the restaurant. Except for the waitress at the back and the two tables with farmers in John Deere hats, there was nobody else to be seen.

"Just once," Tom said, "I'd like to be in a conversation with you that makes sense."

"Shoe check," Johnny said.

"See what I mean?"

"It's part of your education," Johnny said. "Shoe check means everybody at the table pushes back their chairs and looks at their shoes."

"I don't want to ask," Tom said, "but I don't see any choice. Why does everybody push back their chairs and look at their shoes?"

"To see if there is ketchup on the toes of their shoes."

"Weird."

"Not weird," Johnny said. "A trick. If you have ketchup on your toes, everybody laughs at you because you were dumb enough to let someone put ketchup on your shoes."

"Ketchup on shoes?"

"Just on the toes, where you can wipe it off. Better than Toronto, where people put it on someone's coat."

"I already explained that coat check means you leave your coat at—"

"Shoe check," Johnny said. Johnny pushed back his chair. "My shoes are clean."

"Fine," Tom said. He pushed back his chair. "If it makes you feel better I'll check my..."

Tom frowned again as he looked down. "Hey, there's ketchup on my toes."

Johnny started to laugh. "Great trick, huh?"

Tom's face looked like he had sucked on a lemon. "How did ketchup get on my shoes?"

That's when their friend, Stu Duncan, crawled out from under the table with a bottle of ketchup.

"Hi, Tom," Stu said. "Johnny's right. You sure have a lot to learn. Good thing we are here to help you get ready for the Wassabee."

SPECIALS

Chapter Two
Road Trip!

Just then Mrs. Green, the waitress, brought three orders of French fries. She set them on the table.

"Thanks," Stu said. He shook the ketchup bottle. "Could we have more? This one is empty."

Mrs. Green nodded. "I saw you under the table. Who got shoe-checked?"

"Not me," Johnny said.

"Not me," Stu said.

"That leaves you," Mrs. Green said to Tom. She shook her head in sympathy for Tom. "But you're new to town. Better luck next time."

Mrs. Green went for more ketchup.

Stu put a French fry in each of his nostrils and stared at Tom. The French fries looked like tusks sticking out of Stu's face. Stu looked like a walrus. "Don't take it personally. This is training. We're trying to get you ready for the Wassabee."

Tom sighed. "Why me?"

"You should feel lucky," Johnny said. "Not everybody gets to play in the legendary Wassabee. It's two weeks away, and we need to start getting ready for it."

"I didn't even hear about it until today," Tom said. "Until you phoned and said we needed to meet here to talk about it. What is the Wannabee anyway?"

Johnny stared at Tom in horror.

Stu stared at Tom in horror. One of the French fries fell from Stu's nose onto the table. Now he looked like a walrus with a broken tusk.

"What?" Tom said. "What did I do?"

"You mocked the Wassabee," Stu said. He picked up the French fry and ate it.

"Yes," Johnny said, "it's not the Wannabee. It's the Wassabee. WHA. SAH. BEE. Never, ever, ever let anyone know that you made fun of it."

Mrs. Green returned with the ketchup. She looked at the other French fry in Stu's nose, but didn't say anything. She walked away.

Stu put ketchup on his plate. He took the French fry from his nose and dipped it in the ketchup. He offered it to Tom.

Tom sighed again and shook his head.

Stu shrugged and ate the French fry.

"Tell me about the WHA-SAH-BEE," Tom said. "Is it some kind of Egyptian curse, like I'll be swarmed with frogs for saying it wrong?"

Johnny stared at Tom in horror. "You're mocking it again."

Stu stared at Tom in horror. "Johnny, if this keeps up, I may lose my appetite."

Stu grabbed another French fry. "But then again, maybe not."

"The Wassabee is the annual fathers-against-sons hockey game," Johnny explained. "The winning team gets the Wassabee trophy and bragging rights for the rest of the year."

"Yahoo," Tom said. "Just thinking about it gives me chills. In a town this big, there must be, what, two entire teams? The fathers and the sons? So if we lose, we still finish second in all of Howling."

"He's still mocking it," Stu said. "Make him stop."

"There's a couple of things you don't know about the Wassabee," Johnny told Tom. "First, it's always played out of town. At a winter camp. On outdoor ice. On Lake Wassabee."

"That's four things already," Tom said.

"Focus," Johnny said. "I haven't got to the first one yet."

"But—"

Johnny interrupted Tom. "First. Because it's out of town, there are no women allowed. Ever."

"It's a road trip," Stu said. "Always remember, what goes on the road, stays on the road. The only thing the mothers ever learn is who won. Not what happened."

"Like shoe checks, I suppose," Tom said.

"See," Johnny grinned. "I knew you'd catch on fast."

"Anything else?" Tom said. "You know, while I'm getting so excited about this."

"One last thing," Johnny said. "There are two ways to score points. On the ice. And off."

"Off? How do you score a goal from off the ice?"

"That's the fun part," Johnny said. "We call them Wassabee points. Trust me. You'll learn."

Chapter Three
The First Wassabee Point

The next Saturday afternoon, Tom stepped into the kitchen at Stu's house. Johnny and Stu were already sitting at the kitchen table. Stu held a black marker. There were sheets of paper on the table. There was a small camera on the table too.

"Guys," Tom said. "What's up?"

"Getting ready for the Wassabee," Stu answered. Stu said to Johnny, "I'm so great, I'm jealous of myself."

"Not good enough."

"When I was born, I was so surprised, I didn't talk for a year."

"Nope," Johnny said. "Still not good enough."

"I stopped to think and forgot to get started again."

Tom began to frown. "This is getting ready for the Wassabee?"

"Yes," Johnny said, "how about this, Stu? Four out of three people have trouble with fractions."

"Huh?" Tom said.

"That doesn't make sense," Stu said. "Four out of three people have trouble with fractions?"

Stu thought about it. A second later, he said, "Oh, I get it. Very funny."

Johnny grinned. "Or this: There are three kinds of people in this world. Those who can count. And those who can't."

"Huh?" Tom said again. "Will one of you tell me how this is getting ready for the Wassabee?"

"Hang on," Stu said. "Johnny, you said three kinds of people, but you only counted two kinds. Oh, I get it. That's funny too."

"Funny enough for a sign?" Johnny asked.

"No," Stu said, "that takes too much thinking."

"Please, please, please," Tom said. "Make sense!"

"Shhh," Stu said. "My dad is in the living room. On the couch. Watching golf. Don't wake him up."

"How can he be watching golf if he's asleep?"

"Have you ever watched golf?" Stu answered.

"I see your point." Tom nodded. "But why don't you want to wake him up?"

"We need to score the first Wassabee point," Johnny told Tom. "Remember, we leave next Friday, right after school."

"You told me that playing a trick was like scoring a goal. This doesn't look like a trick."

"Not yet," Johnny answered Tom. Johnny turned to Stu. "How's this then?"

Johnny took a marker. He began writing on a sheet of paper. He used big bold letters and printed something for Tom and Stu to read. He also drew a big arrow pointing at the edge of the page.

"I like it," Stu said. "I like it a lot."

"I still don't get it," Tom said, frowning at the sign.

"You mean I have to explain what it means?" Johnny said. "I thought you were smarter than that."

"I mean I don't get what you are doing." Tom moaned. "Why did my parents have to move to Howling from Toronto?"

"So people wouldn't put ketchup on your coat in a restaurant," Johnny said. "How can anyone live in a cruel city like that?"

Tom moaned again.

Stu patted Tom's back. "Tom, it will be okay. Just wait here. But be quiet."

Stu picked up the camera. Johnny picked up the sheet of paper. Tom sat at the table as Stu and Johnny tiptoed to the living room. But for Stu, it wasn't exactly tiptoeing. Stu always ate a lot of French fries.

Less than a minute later, Stu and Johnny tiptoed back into the kitchen.

"Perfect," Stu said. "Dad was fast asleep."

"He snores like you," Johnny said. "At least I hope that was snoring. It did smell bad in there."

"Ha, ha," Stu said.

"Please tell me what's going on," Tom said.

"I'll show you instead." Johnny turned the camera around so Tom could see the photo they had just taken of Stu's dad.

It was a close-up of his head. His eyes were closed. The sign Johnny had made was right beside Stu's dad's head.

"What do you think?" Johnny said. "Will this photo be worth a Wassabee point?"

Tom finally understood why Johnny had drawn the arrow on the paper. He smiled. "Yes, and for the first time, I'll admit I'm glad to be part of the Wassabee. It's going to be fun, isn't it."

"Only if we win," Stu said.

Tom looked at the photo one more time and smiled again.

I'M THE BOSS MY WIFE SAID I COULD BE!

The arrow pointed at Stu's dad's head. In big bold letters, the sign said: *I'M THE BOSS. MY WIFE SAID I COULD BE!*

Chapter Four
Emergency Food Stop

It was Friday. The beginning of the legendary Wassabee weekend. All the fathers and all the boys of the Howling Timberwolves stopped at a restaurant along the highway. They were halfway to Wassabee Lake.

The fathers went inside first. The boys on the team were wearing their Howling Timberwolves team jackets.

"I love this restaurant," Stu said to Johnny.

"Let me guess," Tom said. "It has an all-you-can-eat buffet."

"Take my advice and stuff yourself," Stu said. "The dads are cooking at Lake Wassabee. All weekend. This is your last chance for civilized food until we get back to Howling."

"Yeah," Johnny said. "Remember last year? One of the dads left a can of baked beans on the woodstove while we played hockey. It exploded. There were beans everywhere."

"I don't remember," Stu said.

Johnny elbowed Tom. "He doesn't want to remember. We caught him scraping beans off the wall with a spoon."

"Nothing surprises me anymore," Tom said. "Nothing."

"I hope it stays that way," Johnny told him. "The dads are going to try to spring surprises on us all weekend."

"But no matter what happens," Stu said, "don't forget. What goes on the road, stays on the road."

"Like last year," Johnny said, "when my dad crawled under a table with a ketchup bottle to do a shoe-check trick on us. Except we saw him crawl under it."

Stu laughed. "I remember that. We switched tables with some truckers, so they sat at the booth instead of us. Johnny's dad didn't dare move for the

whole meal. We counted that as a Wassabee point for us."

"I never heard about that." Tom shook his head.

Stu giggled. "And you never heard that the truckers accidentally kicked him at the end of the meal. They didn't think it was funny when they caught him under the table. We did though. We counted that as another Wassabee point."

"I never heard about that either." Tom kept shaking his head as if he couldn't believe it.

"Neither did my mom," Johnny said. "Even though I really wanted to tell her."

"What goes on the road, stays on the road," Stu reminded Tom. "That's part of the Wassabee weekend."

Johnny smiled. "Including the best shoe check in all of history. Coming up next."

Johnny and Stu looked at Tom.

Tom nodded. "Don't worry. I have the water pistol right here in my pocket."

Chapter Five
World's Best Shoe Check

In the restaurant, all the players on the Howling Timberwolves team sat at one long table. All the fathers sat at another table. Everybody ordered the buffet. Everybody stood up to go to the buffet table.

Tom pulled out his water pistol. He walked up behind his dad. He squirted his dad on the back of the neck.

"Hey!" Tom's dad turned around. "What are you doing?"

All the dads looked over. They saw Tom with the water pistol.

"Wassabee!" Tom said. "It's worth a point, right?"

"I don't think so," Tom's dad said. "That wasn't much of a trick."

Tom squirted the water right in his dad's eyes. "Is that better?"

His dad got mad. "No! Don't do that again. Even if this is the Wassabee weekend."

"Come on," Tom answered. "It should be worth a point. Maybe we could vote on it."

All of the dads were shaking their heads against Tom's idea.

"Oh well," Tom said. "Maybe next time I'll do better."

The dads walked to the buffet table and lined up with all the other people.

"Good job," Stu whispered to Tom. "It worked. All the dads were watching you. None of them saw Johnny crawl under the buffet table."

Stu and Tom were standing at the end of the buffet line. They saw what nobody else saw.

TORONTO
MAPLE LEAFS

The buffet table had a tablecloth that stretched to the floor. As each dad passed the spot where Johnny was hiding under the table, Johnny lifted the cloth a little. Then he reached out and squirted ketchup on top of all the dads' shoes.

After the last dad passed him, Johnny let the tablecloth fall back down to the floor. A few seconds later, he reached the end of the buffet table, near Tom and Stu. He crawled out.

"Is it safe to stand?" Johnny asked.

"No one is looking," Stu answered.

"Good." Johnny stood up and joined Stu and Tom. They passed through the buffet line and filled their plates. Stu filled two plates.

"Good work," Stu said. "You just made history. You got ketchup on everybody's shoes."

"He means *everybody*," Tom said. "You got a few of the other people in line too."

"Oops," Johnny said. "All I could see was the size of the shoes. Not the people in them."

They walked back to their table. Stu finished both his plates before Johnny and Tom could finish one plate each. Stu went back for thirds.

Finally the meal was over.

Johnny and Tom and Stu walked to the table with all the dads.

"Wassabee point," Johnny said to the dads. He threw a photo on the table. It was the photo of Stu's dad asleep. With the sign that said: *I'M THE BOSS. MY WIFE SAID I COULD BE!*

All the dads began to laugh. Especially Stu's dad. He laughed the loudest.

"All right, all right," Johnny's dad said. "That is worth one point. Your team is now up one to nothing."

All the boys on the Timberwolves team clapped.

The other people in the restaurant stared at them. After the clapping stopped, it was quiet. Then someone from another table said really loudly, "Hey! Why is there ketchup on my shoes?"

“Pretty funny,” Johnny’s dad said. “I guess other people play the shoe-check trick on each other too.”

“Maybe all you dads should do a shoe check,” Johnny said. “For the first time in Wassabee history, we were able to shoe-check everybody at the table.”

“Impossible!” his dad said. “We looked under the table to make sure no one was there.”

“Impossible?” Johnny repeated. “Then I guess you won’t mind doing a shoe check. If I’m wrong, your team gets two Wassabee points. If I’m right, we get two points.”

All the dads pushed back their chairs. All the dads looked down at their shoes. All the dads groaned.

“Three to nothing for us,” Johnny said. All the Howling Timberwolves clapped again. “Good luck with the rest of your weekend!”

Chapter Six
Nightmares!

In his sleeping bag, in the dark, Johnny dreamed of exploding marshmallows.

There was a reason for this. Before going to bed, the fathers had built a fire for a marshmallow roast. The boys had thought this was great. Until the marshmallows had begun to explode, sending them running.

The fathers had laughed and laughed. They had put popcorn kernels in the marshmallows. It had given them a Wassabee point. But the boys were still winning three to one, and Johnny had fallen asleep with a smile on his face.

His dreams changed from exploding marshmallows to dreams about mice crawling on his body. He did not enjoy these dreams. He woke up.

There was a problem though. He was still dreaming about mice crawling on his body.

Johnny wondered how he could still be dreaming if he was awake.

Maybe he was dreaming that he was awake. He blinked his eyes a few times to see if he was awake or asleep. He was in a cabin with bunk beds and a woodstove. The stove was burning firewood to heat the cabin. He could see the glow of the fire inside the stove.

He could also hear Stu snoring on the bunk bed below him. Johnny knew he was awake.

Except it still felt like mice were crawling along his body.

Then Johnny realized something. Mice *were* crawling along his body! Inside his sleeping bag!

He wanted to scream. But he was afraid if he moved, the mice would bite him. So he stayed as still as he could.

Then Stu's snoring stopped.

"Are you awake?" Johnny whispered.

"Yes," Stu said, "but I wish I wasn't. It feels like there are mice in my sleeping bag."

"Me too," Johnny said. "But I'm afraid if I move they will bite me."

"Me too," Stu said. "This is horrible."

"What do we do?" Johnny asked.

"First I have to tell you something," Stu said.

"What?"

Before Stu could answer, loud school bells surprised them. Very loud school bells. It was as if there were hundreds of them.

Chapter Seven
Trapped in a Sleeping Bag

It was so loud Johnny jumped inside his sleeping bag. The mice scurried up his body and into his armpits. He screamed and jumped some more. But the school bells were louder than his screaming.

The mice jumped onto his face.

Johnny screamed again. He fought the sleeping bag, trying to get out. But he was stuck inside the sleeping bag.

He rolled and fought and screamed.

He rolled right out of the top bunk!

He screamed again.

He landed on something soft. It was Stu.

BRRRNG!

Johnny rolled onto the floor. He was still in his sleeping bag. The good news was it seemed like all the mice had left his sleeping bag. The bad news was the school bells were still ringing really loudly.

The other boys in the cabin had found their flashlights. They were looking for the school bells.

They finally found what was making the noise. Alarm clocks.

There were alarm clocks everywhere in the cabin. And all of the alarm clocks were ringing.

Tom had an alarm clock in his hand. He threw it into the fire in the stove in the middle of the cabin. The alarm clock stopped ringing.

Then big flashlight beams suddenly filled the cabin.

The fathers had arrived. They shone their flashlights on all the boys.

The fathers were laughing very hard.

"Wassabee! Wassabee!" Tom's dad said. "How's that for a trick? Better than squirting water in your eyes?"

The other alarm clocks had finally stopped ringing.

One of the fathers pointed a flashlight at Johnny. He was still stuck in his sleeping bag. On the floor. Where he had fallen after rolling off of Stu.

"Did the birdseed trick work?" Johnny's dad asked.

"Birdseed?" Johnny said.

"In your sleeping bag. Did mice go inside your sleeping bag to look for the birdseed?"

"Yes," Johnny had to admit.

"Wassabee!" his dad shouted. "Wassabee! More points for us!"

Johnny tried to get out of his sleeping bag. That's when he noticed a safety pin. It had pinned his T-shirt to the inside of the sleeping bag.

"I suppose you did this too?" he asked his dad.

"No," his dad said. "But I wish I did."

"Who did it then?" Johnny asked.

"Um," Stu said, "remember a minute ago when I told you there was something you needed to know?"

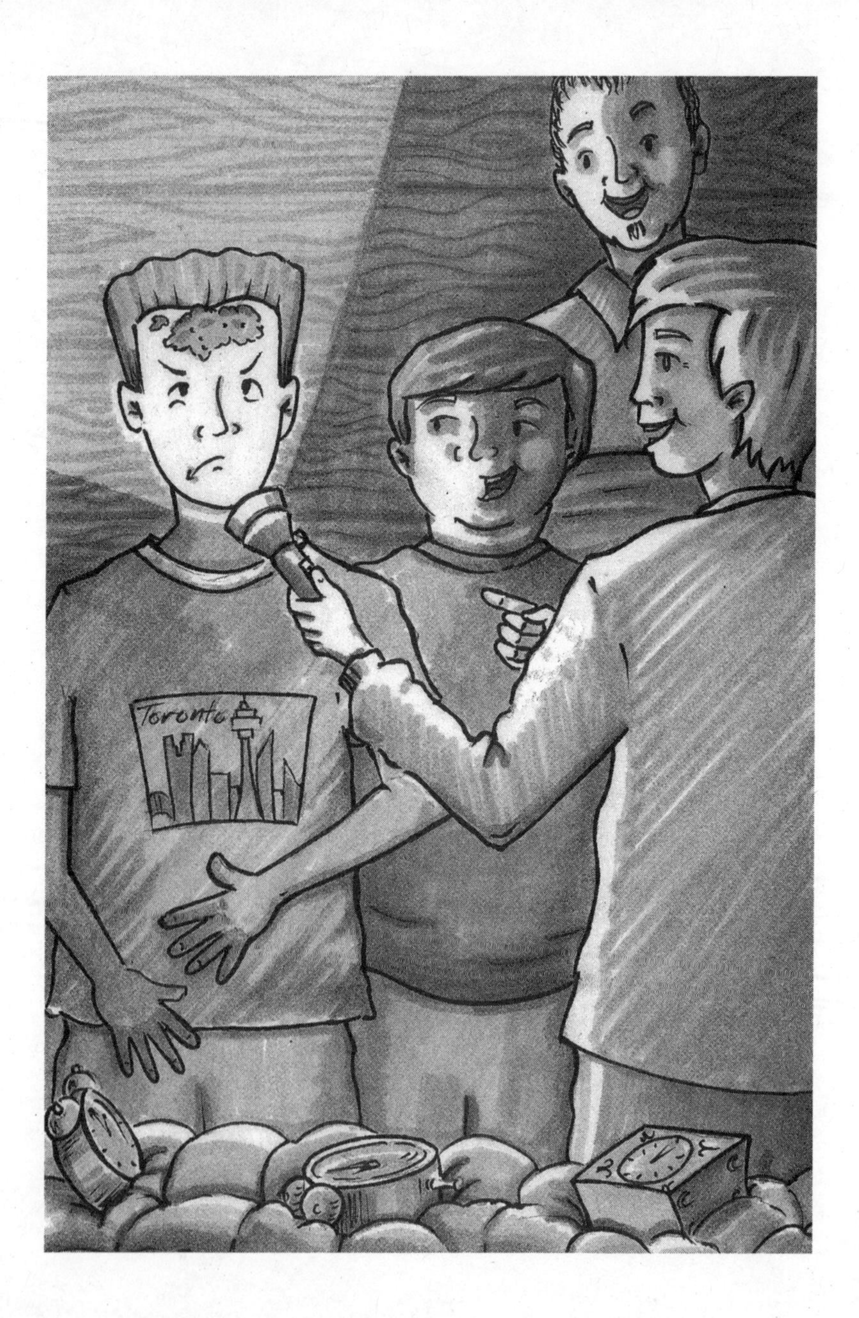
Toronto

"You?" Johnny said. "I can't believe you would play a trick on me."

"Why not?" Stu said. "Last year you put peanut butter on my face while I was sleeping."

Tom started laughing at Johnny.

Johnny found a flashlight and shone it at Tom. There was a big brown blob on Tom's face. Peanut butter. At least that trick had worked again this year.

Chapter Eight
The Big Game

Johnny and Stu and Tom stood on the ice and shivered in their hockey equipment. They were watching the other players on the Howling Timberwolves play the fathers.

Their shift was next. The score was still nothing to nothing. At least the hockey score was nothing to nothing. The Wassabee score was three to three.

"This is crazy," Tom said, stamping his skates. "Do you have any idea how cold it is?"

"No," Johnny said, "I'm not here."

"Huh?

"You asked a dumb question," Johnny said. "I gave you a dumb answer. Of course I know how cold it is. I'm standing right beside you."

Howling
Howling

"On a lake," Stu said sadly. "With wind blowing sideways. And snow in our faces. Worse, there's no hot-dog stand nearby."

Stu was right about all four things. They were on Lake Wassabee. The fathers and the Howling Timberwolves had used snow shovels to clear an area on the ice to play. They had put nets on each end of the cleared area. Behind them was the camp with the cabins. The trucks and vans that the fathers had driven to Lake Wassabee were parked near the cabins.

But the players could barely see the cabins because it had begun to snow so hard.

Worse, one of the fathers just scored a goal.

"Rats," Johnny said. "Now it's four to three for them."

"My toes are cold," Tom said.

"Don't tell the dads," Johnny said. "They'll call you a sissy."

"I *am* a sissy," Tom said. "At least when it comes to the cold. How can we play hockey in these conditions?"

"If we don't," Johnny said, "we'll lose the Wassabee trophy. So are you ready?"

"No," Tom said.

"No," Stu said.

One of the other fathers scored another goal. Now the Timberwolves were down 5–3.

"You better be ready," Johnny said to Tom.

"It's snowing so hard I can barely see," Tom said. "How are we supposed to play in these conditions?"

Tom was right. It was hard to see. That gave Johnny an idea.

"Grab an extra puck," he told Tom. "I think we can score two points with one goal and tie the game."

"Impossible!" Tom said.

"Not in the Wassabee," Johnny answered with a grin. "Let me explain."

Chapter Nine
An Impossible Comeback

Johnny won the draw. The puck went back to Stu on defense. The puck did not move fast. The snow was falling so hard that the ice was sticky.

Tom was on the wing. He skated forward.

Johnny did something strange. He should have skated forward too. He should have gone to an open place on the ice to get a pass from Stu. Instead, Johnny skated back toward his own net.

Stu did something strange too. As one of the fathers skated toward him, he should have passed the puck to the other defense. Or to an open forward. Instead, Stu passed the puck to the Timberwolves goalie.

Johnny skated behind the net.

The goalie used his stick to move the puck around behind the net to Johnny. It was snowing so hard that Johnny could barely see the other net.

"Come and get me!" Johnny yelled to the fathers. "Unless you're afraid I can deke all of you!"

The fathers laughed and charged toward the net.

Johnny dropped his right-hand hockey glove. He reached down for the puck. He made a throwing motion. He yelled, "Tom, long bomb!"

Up ahead on the ice, Tom yelled back. "Got it!"

Tom jumped in the air. He reached way up with one hand. He landed. He dropped his hand to the ice and dropped a puck from his glove.

Breakaway!

Tom raced toward the goalie. It was his dad in net.

Tom lifted his stick to fire a slap shot. His dad jumped a little. His dad knew Tom had a hard slap shot.

But Tom was faking.

Howling

He brought his stick down. He pulled the puck to the left. Then to the right. He fired a low wrist shot into the bottom-right side of the net.

Goal!

"Unfair!" Johnny's dad said.

"Not unfair!" Johnny answered. "This is the Wassabee. Remember?"

"Let them have the goal," Stu's dad said, skating to them. "It won't matter. It's snowing so hard, we're going to have to stop the game."

"What?" Johnny said. "That's unfair."

"No," Stu's dad said, "this is the Wassabee. Remember? Besides, we have to think about the drive home. If it keeps snowing like this, it will be unsafe. And we'll have to go so slow we might not get back in time."

"So you're sure the goal counts?" Johnny said.

"Sure," Johnny's dad answered. "But that means you lose, five to four."

"Wassabee point!" Johnny yelled. He pulled a puck out of his hockey glove. "Wassabee point!"

"What?" his dad said.

"I didn't throw a puck to Tom," Johnny explained. "I only pretended to throw the puck. The whole time, Tom had a different puck in his own glove. He pretended to catch it, and used the puck he already had. You couldn't see the trick because it was snowing so hard."

"Wassabee point!" Tom yelled.

"Wassabee point!" Stu yelled.

All together, the rest of the Timberwolves started yelling too. "Wassabee! Wassabee! Wassabee! Wassabee! Wassabee!"

Finally the dads started laughing. Johnny's dad waved his hands for silence.

"Okay, okay. That was worth a Wassabee point. The game is tied. Nobody wins this year, right?"

But it turned out Johnny's dad was wrong.

Howling

Chapter Ten
Mystery Revenge

Johnny was scraping snow off the windshield of the van as Tom's dad sat behind the steering wheel. Tom's dad started the van to warm up the engine as guys loaded gear into the back.

When the engine started, Johnny saw something strange.

Snow inside the van. Snow everywhere. It looked like a snow globe that someone had turned upside down and shaken.

Johnny didn't understand until Tom's dad jumped out of the van. His clothes were covered in confetti. His hair was full of confetti. There was confetti stuck in his eyebrows.

Tom's dad tried to yell. He stopped. He spit confetti from his mouth.

"Hey, who did that!" he finally yelled. "Who put confetti in the fans!"

Johnny figured it out. One of the Timberwolves must have poured confetti in the vents of the van. When Tom's dad turned on the fan to defrost the windows, the confetti had blown all over him.

And all over the inside of the van.

Johnny thought that was a great trick.

"Wassabee point!" Johnny yelled. "Wassabee point!"

Nearly all the Howling Timberwolves thought it was a great trick too. "Wassabee point! Wassabee point! Wassabee point!"

The only Howling Timberwolf who did not think it was a great trick was Tom.

"Tom," his dad yelled. "You're going to have to clean up the van as soon as we get home. If I find even one piece of confetti, you lose your allowance."

The other dads came over from their trucks and cars. They had confetti in their hair and eyebrows too.

"Wassabee point! Wassabee point! Wassabee point!" yelled Johnny.

"Okay, okay, okay," Johnny's dad said. "You are up one point. But remember, it's a long drive home. We still have time to get you back."

Everyone got into the vans and trucks and cars to drive away from the cabins at Camp Wassabee. But the tricks weren't over.

Chapter Eleven
The Biggest Surprise

Johnny and Stu and Tom were in the back of the van.

"Great trick," Tom said as he looked at all the confetti around him. It didn't sound like he meant it. "I'll never get this clean. There goes my allowance."

"It was great," Johnny said. "When we get back to Howling, I'm going to find out which one of the guys on the team thought of it. As long as nothing happens at the restaurant on the way home, we have won the Wassabee."

"Rest-oh-rant," Stu said, like he was kissing the word. Every year the fathers and sons stopped at the same restaurant on the way home. The food was never very good at Camp Wassabee.

"Hey!" Tom's dad said from the front. "What's wrong?"

Nobody answered. Tom's dad was talking to himself. He was pushing hard on the gas pedal, but the van was not moving.

"We must be stuck," he said. "All this snow."

But he was wrong.

Everybody got out to push the van.

Johnny noticed it first. "The tires aren't touching the ground."

Tom dropped to his knees and looked underneath. "You're right. Someone put blocks of wood underneath the axle."

"What a great trick!" Johnny said. "Wassabee point."

All the Howling Timberwolves yelled again. "Wassabee point! Wassabee point! Wassabee point!"

It didn't take them long to find out that all the cars and vans were on blocks of wood. But it took the dads a few minutes to jack up the cars and vans

and pull out the blocks. Now they were covered in confetti and in more snow.

Johnny thought this was funny. The dads did not think it was funny. In the two hours it took to drive to the restaurant in the snow, the dads did not talk much.

But there was one more surprise. The biggest one of all.

Chapter Twelve
Final Shoe Check

When the dads and the boys walked into the restaurant, they saw all the moms at a table in the back.

"What are they doing here?" Johnny said.

"They must have really missed us," Johnny's dad said.

But Johnny's dad was wrong.

As soon as the moms saw the dads and the Howling Timberwolves, they all yelled, "Wassabee points! Wassabee points! Wassabee points!"

They didn't care that other people in the restaurant were staring at them.

All the moms began to laugh.

"Did you like the confetti?" Johnny's mom asked. "That was my idea."

"Did you like the blocks of wood under the axles?" Tom's mom asked. "That was my idea."

"You?" Johnny's dad said. "You did that to us?"

"It was a long drive, but it was worth it," Stu's mom said. "It was my idea to play Wassabee tricks on you. We had the spare keys to get into your cars and vans. We did it while you were on the ice playing the big game."

"Why?" Stu's dad said.

"Boys aren't the only ones who can go on the road," she answered. "You were right. Wassabee points are fun."

The dads didn't say anything. They just stared at the ground. The moms had really fooled them.

Johnny said, "Too bad you can't tell anybody in Howling about this. Remember, what goes on the road, stays on the road."

"That's right," Johnny's dad said. He started smiling again. All the dads looked much happier now that the moms' Wassabee points would be kept

a secret from all their friends in Howling. "Thanks for reminding us, Johnny."

"Time for the buffet?" Stu asked. "Please?"

Everybody laughed. The moms got up to go to the buffet table.

Everybody got in line at the buffet table.

Except for Johnny. He stayed behind. He made sure no one was looking, grabbed a bottle of ketchup and crawled under the table where the moms were going to eat.

If they wanted to be part of the Wassabee, he thought, it was time for them to learn about shoe checks.

Sigmund Brouwer is the best-selling author of many books for children and young adults. Sigmund loves visiting schools and talking to children about reading and writing. *Timberwolf Tracks* is his sixth book about the Timberwolves. The other books in the series are: *Timberwolf Challenge*, *Timberwolf Chase*, *Timberwolf Hunt*, *Timberwolf Revenge* and *Timberwolf Trap*.